THE CASE OF THE MISSING BURGER (WITH THE BUN)
BY

Angela Mae Morrison-AKA Darnell

Kindle   direct
                Publishing

1

Kindle   Direct
                              Publishing

First published 2025
Kindle Direct Publishing (UK Office)
 Edited by: Claudette Leckie (USA)
 Edited by: Jamila Morrison (UK)

ACKNOWLEDGEMENTS

I would like to express my deepest gratitude to my husband, Roy Morrison, for his unwavering love, support, encouragement, and invaluable input throughout the writing of this book.

To my two sons, Dalmar and Ryan, thank you for always stepping in to help with technical challenges, often at a moment's notice.

A special thanks to my sister Claudette in the USA, whose editorial support was both timely and thoughtful.

And finally, to my daughter Jamila, I am especially grateful for the time and energy she dedicated, despite her busy schedule, to assist with various aspects of this book, including editing. Your contributions meant so much.

ABOUT THE AUTHOR

Angela Mae Morrison is a dedicated registered nurse with a wealth of experience in healthcare and a deep-rooted passion for storytelling. She earned her nursing qualifications from Wolverhampton University and Birmingham City University, and has spent years serving patients with compassion, professionalism, and care.

Currently working part-time as a nurse, Angela balances her clinical career with her lifelong love for writing. Inspired by everyday experiences, family life, and the subtle humour and mysteries hidden in ordinary moments, she brings a fresh and heartfelt perspective to her stories.

Angela lives in Birmingham, England, with her husband Roy and their children. When she's not caring for patients or crafting new tales, she enjoys quiet moments with family, reading, baking, and reflecting on the joys and challenges of modern life.

Her writing is a blend of warmth, wit, and realism, often inspired by real events and shaped by her unique lens as both a nurse and a mother. Whether she's solving household mysteries or capturing the emotions of family life, Angela invites readers into stories that feel familiar yet are full of unexpected twists.

Books published by Angela Mae Morrison-AKA Darnell

My Weight Loss Journey Throughout Lockdown 2022
Publisher: Olympia Publisher, London 2022

Coming Out of A Dark Place;
A true-life story about mental endurance through challenging times.
KDP Publishing 2023.

My Diet Log
A journal about maintaining healthy eating and calorie counting.
(KDP Publishing 2023)

Everyday Poetry
Poems about everyday living
(KDP Publishing 2023)

Sunny and Moonie
A children's book about the Sunny and the Moonie adventures
Educational book about the sun and the moon.

(KDP Publishing 2024)

Sunny and Moonie Part 2- *Their adventure continued* in *outer space and beyond.*
(KDP Publishing 2024)
Sunny and Moonie colouring book

 Mother Hen and her twelve chicks-

Check out Angie's YouTube channel (you can find it
@angiemorrison3910;

Angie's TikToc@angelamorrison419.

INTRODUCTION

THE CASE OF THE MISSING BURGER
(with the bun)

This story is inspired by true events, though some names, places, and situations have been fictionalised for creative purposes. While the central mystery remains rooted in reality, a few twists and turns are purely imaginative.

The Case of the Missing Burger follows young Tommy and the puzzling disappearance of his beloved burger, complete with the bun. That night before, Tommy's mom had made him four delicious burgers for dinner. They were so big that he could only manage to eat three. Carefully wrapping up the fourth, he tucked it into the fridge, planning to enjoy it the next day while gaming on his PS5 with friends.

But when the next day arrived, disaster struck; the burger was gone. Vanished. No one in the household could explain its mysterious disappearance. Suspicious and determined, Tommy took matters into his own hands. What started as a simple snack plan quickly turned into a full-blown investigation, full of unexpected clues, unlikely suspects, and more questions than answers.

So, who took Tommy's burger (with the bun)? Can Detective Tommy crack the case and bring the guilty party to justice? Get ready to follow the clues and help solve *The Case of the Missing Burger.*

WHERE IS MY BURGER?
(with the bun)

Hello. My name is Tommy, and today I'm sharing the unbelievable yet entirely true story of a missing burger... complete with its bun.

You might be asking, "Can a burger really go *missing?*" I get it, it sounds funny. Ridiculous, even. But believe me, what happened that day was no joke. The burger was real. The hunger was real. And the mystery? Oh, that was very real.

Now, before you jump to conclusions, let me explain what makes this case so strange. Did the burger somehow walk out of the fridge on its own? Highly unlikely, unless burgers have legs now (which would be a *whole* different kind of story). Was it *moved* by someone? That seems far more plausible.

Let's go over the list of suspects.

First, there's Mylo, our family cat. Yesterday, I caught him staring at my burger like it was a mouse in a sesame seed disguise. He may act innocent, but I've seen him leap onto the kitchen counter like a ninja in the night. Could Mylo be the culprit?

Then there's my sister, Onetta. She doesn't even like burgers, says they're too "greasy." *But*, she's the kind of person who might throw it away just to get it out of the fridge, or worse, feed it to the neighbour's dogs for some strange reason. I wouldn't put it past her.

I love my family, truly, I do, but when it comes to this case, I trust *no one*. Not Mylo. Not Onetta. Not even my loving parents. This was *my* burger, and now it's gone. If I want justice, I'll have to take the case into my own hands.

Call me Detective Tommy. This mystery has my full attention. I've got a notebook, a magnifying glass, and a hunger for both answers *and* burgers.

But before we dive into the investigation, let's rewind a bit. Let me make one thing clear: I *love* burgers. I don't just like them, I *adore* them. If I could eat a burger every single day, I would. No hesitation. Burgers are my ultimate comfort food. They're warm, juicy, and reliable, kind of like a best friend you can chew.

Don't get me wrong, I eat other foods too. Not always willingly, though. My mom insists I "expand my palate," which is her fancy way of saying I have to try stuff I don't want. She's always going on about vitamins, nutrients, and food groups.

"Tommy," she says, "you can't live on burgers forever."

(Spoiler alert: I *can*. I just need a good hiding spot for the wrappers.)

Still, I try to be a good sport. I'll eat chicken. Macaroni and cheese. Baked beans. Tuna with mayonnaise is probably my second-favourite food. Add garlic bread, and it's practically a party. But no matter what new dish Mom puts on my plate, I always come back to my one true love: the burger.

Speaking of love, let me mention McDonald's, the holy land of burgers. Who *doesn't* love McDonald's? Back in the day, I used to beg Mom for a Big Mac every weekend. That was the dream. But of course, Mom had to ruin it with her "rules."

"Tommy," she warned, "no more McDonald's every weekend. Once a month, that's it!"

Ugh. *Once a month.* That's burger torture. But I've learned to adapt. I count down the days. And when the end of the month arrives? Oh, I make *sure* she remembers her promise. Mackie time, baby.

Anyway, this story isn't about fast food; it's about *my* homemade, fridge-chilled, carefully saved burger. The one Mom made with love (and maybe a little salt). The one I didn't get to eat, because someone stole it.

And now, it's time to solve the mystery.

Okay, let's get back to the main event: the mystery of my missing burger (with the bun).

It all began on what seemed like a regular day. That evening, Mom made burgers for dinner, four of them.

Four glorious, golden-brown, juicy burgers. She placed them on a plate, still steaming, and said something that instantly made my stomach drop.

"Tommy," she said, "please leave one for your brother."

Wait, *what?*

I blinked at her like she'd just said the sky was green. "You mean these four burgers, the ones clearly made for *me*, I have to share?"

Now, let me explain. I have two siblings. My big brother Johnny, who's older and taller and always busy doing "important big brother things." And then there's Onetta, my sister, the middle child, who doesn't like burgers and won't even touch them unless you coat them in glitter (and maybe not even then). And then there's me, the youngest, and obviously the one with the best taste in food.

Usually, Mom makes eight burgers: four for Johnny, four for me. Onetta doesn't count; she's never been part of the burger deal. So, when only four showed up that night, I assumed, *naturally,* they were all mine.

But Mom had other plans.

Still, because I'm a good kid (and didn't want to be banned from burgers for life), I muttered a reluctant, "Okay." I figured I'd eat three, and if Johnny wanted the last one, fine. I'd be the bigger person.

Later that evening, Johnny came home and walked into the kitchen. Mom told him there was one burger left with his name on it.

"Just one?" he said, raising an eyebrow. "Nah, I'll pass."

Now *that* was music to my ears.

"Yes!" I whispered under my breath. The burger was officially mine again. No sharing. Just me and my fourth burger, destined to be reunited.

After devouring the first three, I sat back in my chair, feeling like a king after a feast. Mom glanced over at me with a smile.

"You struggling to finish that last burger, son?"

"A little," I admitted, patting my stomach.

She laughed. "Why don't you share it with Mylo? He's been eyeing you up all evening. You know you're his favourite."

"Mom," I said, dead serious.

"You just gave him dinner. He had fish. He's fine. And you know   I don't share burgers, not even with Mylo." She rolled her eyes, still smiling, and left me to it. So, I wrapped up my precious fourth burger *bun and all* and began the preservation process. This wasn't just storage. This was a strategy.

I placed the burger on a white paper plate, slid it carefully into a small plastic bag, and sealed it tightly. Then I opened the fridge and gently set it down on the second shelf, right-hand corner. Prime location. Easy to see. Easy to grab. My burger was safe. Protected. Waiting. Tomorrow, while gaming with my friends on the PS5, I will retrieve it, heat it, and enjoy the perfect snack.

This was Day One.

Later that night, I got a bit peckish, the kind of hunger that sneaks up on you when you're lying in bed. I thought about the burger, so close, just downstairs in the fridge, calling my name. But no. I stayed strong. I made myself a hot chocolate instead (also one of my favourite things in the world) and went to bed.

I even dreamed about the burger. That's how much I loved it. Little did I know…. It would never be there in the morning

THE MISSING BURGER
(With the bun)

The next day, I woke up late. It was the summer holidays, no school, no alarms, no homework, and almost no chores. Just how I like it. The sun was pouring in through my window, casting long golden streaks across the room. Outside, the breeze was cool and soft, like nature telling me, "Take it easy, Tommy." I stretched like a cat and rolled out of bed. No rush. No reason to hurry. All I had planned for the day was some light hoovering (because Mom insists I do at least *something*) and a lot of PS5. It was going to be one of those perfect lazy days.

But more than anything, I was thinking about *my burger*. Yes, the same one I had carefully stored in the fridge the night before. The one with the soft bun, the juicy patty, and all the toppings still intact. Just the thought of it made my mouth water. I had the entire day planned out: gaming with friends online, and halfway through, a burger break. Perfection.

As I wandered into the kitchen, already imagining that first bite, something unexpected happened.

"Tommy," Dad said, looking a little lost, "can you give me a hand with the new washing machine?"

I paused. Normally, laundry was not part of my summer break agenda. But this was no ordinary washing machine; this one came with **Wi-Fi**. That changed everything.

"Sure, Dad," I said, trying not to sound too excited. Finally, a chance to show off my tech skills.

I grabbed my iPhone and got straight to work. The machine had its own app, sleek, modern, and just begging to be mastered. I downloaded it in record time and smiled like I'd just cracked a secret code. Then I shared the app link with everyone in the house so they could connect their phones too. I was the first to get it up and running, and honestly? It felt *awesome*.

Dad stood nearby, watching in awe. He's not exactly fond of technology. Wi-Fi-enabled appliances? Not really his thing. So I had to walk him through the setup, connecting the machine, registering the device, and linking it to the household network. I even had to make myself the main user, which secretly made me feel like the boss of laundry. Then came the fun part: loading the machine. I poured in the detergent, tossed in the clothes, and used the app on my phone to choose the wash cycle. With one tap, the machine started whirring, just like magic, except it was *my* magic.

"How cool is that?" I grinned. "I can go for a walk, hit the gym, or even play PS5, and I'll still know when the washing's done."

Dad gave me a proud pat on the shoulder. "Thanks, son. You've got a real knack for this stuff."

I nodded modestly. "Yeah, I know."

Everything was going perfectly. I had helped out, earned some extra brownie points with Dad, and still had the whole day ahead of me. Now all that was left… was the burger.

After setting up the new washing machine like a tech wizard, Dad went straight back to bed. He works night shifts, so daytime is his rest zone. As for me, I was starving. Setting up a smart appliance isn't easy, you know, especially on an empty stomach. And now, it was nearly 3:30 in the afternoon, and I hadn't eaten a thing all day. Time for the moment I'd been waiting for: **my burger**, the one I had lovingly saved from the night before. The one with the perfect bun. My mouth was watering just thinking about it.

I made myself a cup of hot chocolate (you've probably figured out by now that it's one of my favourite drinks, second only to apple juice), grabbed a bottle of water, and added a packet of crisps to my tray. My PS5 was already loaded up, and I had picked my favourite spot on the settee, extra cushions and all. That spot, by the way, is usually Mom's favourite. She practically *owns* that corner of the couch. But today, she was out shopping, which meant victory. The seat was mine.

Everything was perfect. My setup was flawless. I felt like a king preparing for a feast in front of his royal gaming throne.

But then…

I opened the fridge.

No burger.

I blinked. Looked again.

Still no burger.

I checked the second shelf. Then the third. Then the drawers. I even checked behind the milk and under the leftover curry container, but there was nothing.

My burger (with the bun) was gone.

I felt a wave of shock, followed by confusion, followed by a bubbling pot of **pure rage**.

Who, I wondered, in their dismantled little mind, would do something so evil? Who would commit this act of betrayal? My mom was out. My dad had gone back to bed after I helped him. My brother Johnny was at work. That only left *one* other person in the house: **Onetta**.

But before I got to her, I had to rule out Dad. I remembered seeing him near the fridge before he went upstairs. Could he have taken it?

I marched up to his room, knocked once, and barged in. "Dad," I said, shaking his shoulder, "have you seen my burger? The one I left in the fridge last night?"

Dad groaned, his face half-buried in a pillow. "Tommy, why are you waking me up? For a burger?"

"It's *my* burger. I left it right there on a white plate in a plastic bag. It's gone!"

He rubbed his eyes and sighed. "Son, I don't know who took your burger. Ask your mom when she gets back. Please, just let me sleep. I'm working again tonight."

"But"

"When I wake up, we can search the fridge together if it makes you feel better," he mumbled. "Now close the door."

As I walked out, I could hear him muttering to himself, "A burger, missing from the fridge? What's wrong with this child?"

I sighed. No help there.

Next stop: **Onetta**.

I stormed to her room and knocked firmly.

"What?" she yelled through the door.

"Have you seen my burger?"

"Leave me alone!" she shouted. "I don't care about your stupid burger. You probably ate it already and forgot. Now you want Mom to feel sorry for you and buy more. Typical!"

"Wow," I replied, "you don't have to be so horrible. I just asked a simple question!"

"Close my door!" she yelled again, clearly annoyed.

I slammed it, hard, and turned to find *Mylo the cat* behind me, staring with his wide, innocent eyes.

20

"Meow," he said.

"Oh, don't act all cute and innocent, Mylo," I said, pointing an accusing finger.   "You were staring at my burger last night like it was your next big meal. Don't get in my way today. I'm not in the mood to play."

He meowed again and padded down the hall like he didn't have a care in the world.

Reluctantly, I went back downstairs and made myself beans on toast. **Beans on toast.** That's not a snack, that's a sad replacement for what should've been a glorious burger moment. I sat on the settee, surrounded by my cushions, feeling absolutely defeated.

Gaming just wasn't the same.

I logged into my game and joined my friends online, but even they could tell something was off.

"Yo, Tommy," said Billy, "what's up with you? You are playing like a grandad today."

I sighed. "Someone stole my burger."

There was silence. Then laughter.

"Are you serious?" Billy laughed. "A *burger*?"

"Yes, I'm serious!" I shouted. "It was my burger, with the bun! I left it in the fridge, and someone took it."

"Oh man," said Ethan. "Tommy's going to need a private investigator."

"Yeah!" Billy chimed in. "Call in the Burger Detectives!"

They were cracking up. I was *not* amused.

"You guys are the worst," I snapped. "Now shut up and play."

Then I crushed them in the game.

Because anger fuels victory.

But deep down, I wasn't satisfied. Not with a win. Not with beans. Not until I solved the mystery of the **missing burger.**

After finishing the game, which I won (by the way) despite the emotional trauma, I went back to my room. There was nothing else to do now but wait. Wait for Mom to get home. Wait for the truth. Wait for *justice*.

The clock seemed to slow down. I lay on my bed staring at the ceiling, the same thought spinning in my head like a broken record: *Who took my burger?*

Every fifteen minutes or so, I'd get up, walk to the kitchen, and open the fridge again, as if magically, my burger would reappear. But no. Every time I looked, the shelf was still empty.

The white paper plate was gone. The plastic bag? Vanished. No crumbs. No sauce stain. No evidence. *Nothing.*

Whoever took my burger had cleaned up after themselves. Which meant it wasn't an accident. It was a **planned heist.** Back upstairs, I paced around my room, hands behind my back like a detective deep in thought. I even considered drawing a suspect board. Red string, photos, arrows, the whole deal.

Then I heard it. "Meow. "Mylo. I rushed downstairs. There he was by the back door, meowing like he hadn't eaten in years, which is a joke, because Mylo is basically a furry stomach on legs. I gave him his cat food, and he happily dug in. I opened the back door to let him out for his usual lazy stroll. He stepped outside, looked around like he was considering a nap right there on the doorstep, and plopped himself down in a sun patch. Typical Mylo. He doesn't go far. He just likes fresh air and pretending he's wild. Still, he was on my list of suspects. And I wasn't crossing anyone off. Not yet. He may be cute, loyal, and a bit chubby, but let's not forget-this is the same cat who once knocked a chicken leg off the counter and dragged it under the sofa. And yes, Mylo was still under investigation.

Back in my room, I opened my notebook and started jotting down notes for my official case file. I titled it:

"The case of the Missing Burger (with the Bun)"

Investigator: *Detective Tommy Beckford*
Date: *Ongoing.*
Status: *Cold… but heating up*

Prime Suspects:
1. **Dad**: seen near the fridge, denies involvement. Sleepy, but suspicious.
2. **Onetta**: hostile witness. Hates burgers. Hates me asking questions.
3. **Johnny**: not home at the time, but could've eaten it the night before?
4. **Mylo the Cat**: history of food theft. No alibi. Very cute. Too cute?
5. **Mom:** possibly moved it or gave it to someone. Need to wait for questioning.

This was no longer just about a snack. This was about **principle**. Trust. Family. Justice.

I was going to the bottom of this mystery, no matter what it took.

WHO TOOK MY BURGER?
(with the bun)

Finally, I heard the jingle of keys at the front door. **Mom was home**!

I bolted downstairs so fast I nearly missed a step. Out of breath, I skidded into the hallway and called out, "Hi, Mom! Where are the groceries?"

It felt strange. Usually, Mom would call ahead to let me know she needed help unloading the bags. I'm her official grocery assistant, after all. But today, she only had three bags in her hands, and no phone call.

"I didn't do a big shop today," she said, kicking off her shoes. "I had my appointment this afternoon. Remember? I just picked up a few bits on the way home. Besides, this gives you a break; you're always helping me with the groceries," she added with a warm smile.

Normally, that would've made me feel proud. But not today. Today, I was a boy on a mission.

Once she stepped into the kitchen, I didn't waste a second.

"Mom! Have you seen my burger? It's not in the fridge!"

She paused, blinked, then opened the fridge and gave it a good look. "Are you sure you checked thoroughly, son?"

"I looked, Mom. I looked like five times already. Top to bottom, side to side, I even moved the milk."

Mom gave the fridge a once-over anyway, because that's what moms do, and of course, she didn't find it either.

She closed the door gently and said, "I think Johnny might've eaten it last night. You know how he raids the fridge after midnight."

WHAT?!

If Johnny took my burger **without asking**, he'd better prepare for a full Tommy-style confrontation. I was furious. I started pacing in front of the fridge.

Then Mom said something that gave me a glimmer of hope.

"Have you checked *Johnny's* fridge?"

Let me explain: my big brother Johnny has his own **mini-fridge** in his room. He got it two years ago for his birthday, his pride and joy. He keeps his protein shakes, chocolate bars, and "secret" snacks in there. Maybe, just maybe, he stashed my burger in it last night. I darted off and opened his fridge.

Nothing.

Not even a crumb of burger. Just some yoghurt, bottled water, and an open pack of turkey slices. I trudged back to the kitchen, defeated.

"It's not there," I said. "Gone. Like it never existed." Mom raised her eyebrows. "Well, I don't know where else to tell you to look, Tommy. Did you ask your sister?"

"Yes, I did. And she wasn't exactly nice about it. She called me stupid and told me to leave her alone. She said it's 'just a burger'."

Mom sighed and shook her head. "That wasn't kind of her. I'll talk to Onetta later, but you know your sister doesn't even eat meat, she's practically a part-time rabbit."

"She could've given it to Mylo!" I argued. "Or worse, thrown *it in the bin!*"

"Come on, Tommy," Mom said with a tired laugh. "Your sister wouldn't go out of her way to mess with your food. Still, I'll have a quick word with her later. And I'll text Johnny now, just in case he forgot he ate it."

Mom grabbed her phone and typed quickly. Then we waited. It felt like forever. I stood next to her, arms folded, eyes glued to her phone like it was a crystal ball. *Ping!*

Johnny's reply popped up.

"Nope. Didn't eat anything from the fridge last night."

"OH. MY. WORD.

Where. Is. My. Burger!?

"Calm down, Tommy," Mom said, seeing my face turn red with frustration. "We'll ask your dad when he wakes up."

I looked at her sheepishly. "Um… I already asked Dad."

Her eyes widened. **"You what?!** Tommy, did you wake your father up for a *burger?*"

"He was in the fridge this morning! What if he took it before he went back to bed?"

"Tommy!" she said sharply. "Your dad works nights. He just finished a shift this morning, and you woke him up to ask about *leftovers?*"

"He probably went to the gym after work," I muttered under my breath.

"What was that?" Mom asked.

"Nothing."

Mom shook her head in disbelief. "Please, Tommy. It's just a burger."

I stared at her, shocked. "Just a burger?!"

She was losing it. My *own* mother. How could she call my carefully saved, fridge-protected, burger-with-the-bun, **just a burger?**

That's when I started to get suspicious.

Could it have been **Mom?**

She looked calm, too calm. What if she accidentally moved my burger and put it in her lunch bag? She takes her own food to work every day. She even has a second mini cooler bag in the car. Could she have packed it by mistake and eaten it without knowing?

No: *Could she?*

This case wasn't just difficult anymore. It was turning **personal**.

I grabbed my notebook and jotted a new name under the list of suspects.

New Entry:

- **MOM:** Possibly innocent, but suspicious behaviour. Downplayed the burger's importance. Could be covering up for someone, or herself?

I looked around the kitchen one more time.

This mystery was far from solved.

But trust me, Detective Tommy wasn't giving up.

Not until the case of the Missing Burger (with the bun) was it cracked wide open.

DETECTIVE TOMMY

THE INVESTIGATION DEEPENS

I could hear heavy footsteps thumping down the stairs, followed by a familiar groan.

"How's anyone supposed to sleep in this house with all this noise?" Dad muttered, rubbing his eyes and yawning dramatically.

"Tommy, are you still on about that missing burger?"

He reached the bottom step and gave me a tired look.

"Haven't you found it yet?"

I shook my head. "No, Dad. It's still missing. And yes, I already asked Johnny. *Mom texted him.* He said he didn't take it."

Dad sighed, then walked into the kitchen and opened the fridge as if *his* magical fridge powers would suddenly make the burger reappear.

Nope.

At this point, it was no longer just about the burger; it was a puzzle. Everyone in the house denied knowing anything, and I had absolutely no clues. No sauce stains, no crumbs, no wrappers, not even a whisper of cheese. I was frustrated and mystified. This wasn't just food. This was about trust. This was personal.

"You might need a detective, Tommy," Mom said with a chuckle. "It's *The Case of the Missing Burger, with the Bun!*"

She laughed at her own joke, but I didn't even crack a smile.

"It's not funny anymore, Mom," I said, crossing my arms. "Someone took my burger. Unless it grew legs and walked out of the fridge on its own."

"Well," she shrugged, "then you'd better start investigating."

She smiled again and went back to searching the fridge, like she hadn't already done that *three* times today. And still, no burger.

I even checked the bin. I hoped I wouldn't find it there; no one wants to see their prized burger in a pile of eggshells and used teabags, but I had to rule it out. Nothing.

Just some leftover spaghetti and an empty cereal box.

Then I remembered something.

Johnny's fridge. The one Mom and Dad bought him for his birthday, the same one he used to keep in his bedroom, but had recently moved to the conservatory.

I had already checked it once, but maybe I missed something. I raced over to the conservatory, yanked open the little fridge, and inspected every shelf with detective-like precision. The top shelf: protein bars. Middle shelf: orange juice and some suspicious leftover lasagna. Bottom shelf: nothing but half a cucumber.
No burger. Back to the drawing board.

At that point, no one was safe from suspicion. Even Mylo, our usually lazy, fireplace-hugging cat, was on the list.
You're probably wondering: *how can a cat be a suspect?* Can he open the fridge with his paws? Probably not. But I wouldn't put it past someone in this house to sneak him a treat. And what better treat than my burger (with the bun)?
I didn't forget what happened yesterday when he kept following me around, meowing like he wanted a bite. I didn't share it then. Maybe he's holding a grudge. Revenge can be quiet and furry.
Still, I had bigger suspects to focus on.

My **prime suspect** remained **Johnny**, my gym-going, football-playing, fridge-raiding older brother. He's notorious for creeping down in the middle of the night, rummaging through leftovers like a raccoon with protein goals. And if your name isn't written in permanent marker on your food, he treats it like it belongs to the whole house.

Dad even backed up my theory. "I thought maybe Johnny took it," he said, scratching his chin. "Especially after you told him yesterday, he couldn't have it."

"Exactly!" I said, pointing dramatically like a detective in a courtroom drama.

But Mom shook her head. "If Johnny said he didn't eat it, I believe him. He doesn't lie about food."

Ha!

Johnny has a whole history of "not lying" about food, like that time the apple pie disappeared, and he said, "Well, technically, it wasn't labelled."

Let's be clear, unless it's under lock and key or your name on it, Johnny thinks all food is **community property**.

I noticed something else strange, too.

Every time Mom went into the fridge, she kept glancing around like she still expected to find the burger magically hiding behind a bottle of ketchup or tucked behind the butter. She moved things, frowned, and mumbled to herself:

"Where can it be?"

"She's acting weird," I thought. "Suspicious. Almost, guilty."

Could she have eaten it by mistake? Packed it in her lunch and forgot? Or, worse, thrown it out during a fridge clean and blocked it from memory?

My notebook was starting to fill up with suspects.

Suspects List:
- **Johnny:** Prime suspect. Known fridge thief. Midnight snack history.
- **Onetta:** Rude when questioned. Vegetarian alibi is suspiciously convenient.
- **Mom:** Downplaying the burger's importance. Overly smiley. Possibly hiding something.
- **Dad:** Seemed clueless. But it could be a sleeper agent in this operation.
- **Mylo the Cat:** Motivated by revenge. Possibly manipulated by a human accomplice.

This was no longer just about food.
This was about *justice*.
This was about *respect*.
This was about *honour in the kitchen*

And until I solved this mystery, no snack would ever taste the same again.
Not even a burger (with the bun).

NO SIGN OF THE MISSING BURGER
(with the bun)

Still no sign of the missing burger. *With the bun.*

I woke up unusually early, well, early for me, anyway. It was around 12:30 p.m., and the sun was streaming through my window like a spotlight on a crime scene. I blinked a few times, groaned, and stretched. Wednesday mornings are usually peaceful, but not today. Not when a serious food-related mystery was still unsolved.

I sat at my desk and opened my laptop, determined to dig deeper into the case. Maybe I'd missed a clue. Maybe there was a pattern I hadn't seen. Maybe I was turning into a full-time burger detective.

That's when I heard a soft, demanding *meow* just outside my bedroom door.

It was Mylo.

I opened the door, and he strolled in with the same nonchalant attitude he always had, like he owned the place.

"Are you going to help me solve this mystery?" I asked him.

He blinked slowly and stared at me, tail twitching.

"I still don't trust you," I muttered, narrowing my eyes. "My gut says someone gave you my burger. Maybe my sister. Maybe in secret. And you? You just gobbled it up without a trace, didn't you?"

He tilted his head and gave me that innocent look cats are famous for.

I wasn't buying it.

Downstairs, the smell of something delicious drifted up to my room, warm, rich, buttery. My stomach growled like a thunderstorm. Mom was in the kitchen again. **S**he always wakes up early, even on her days off. It's like her body refuses to sleep in.

Today, it smelled like she was baking bread, and not just any bread. *Coco bread.* My sister Onetta's favourite.

Now, if you've never heard of coco bread, let me explain. It's a soft, slightly sweet Caribbean bread, shaped like a folded pillow, and usually served with spicy Jamaican patties or ackee and saltfish. It's the kind of thing that makes your mouth water just thinking about it. I headed downstairs to investigate, not the burger this time, but the heavenly scent.

"*Tommy!*" Mom called from the kitchen. "Still no sign of your missing burger?"

She chuckled. "It's officially *The Case of the Missing Burger (With the Bun).*"

I groaned.

"It's not funny anymore, Mom," I said, my face dropping. "I'm convinced someone took it. I've searched everywhere. The fridge, the bin, Johnny's fridge, again. Still nothing."

Mom glanced up from the oven and sighed. "Where could it possibly be?" she muttered under her breath.

"I'm serious," I said, growing more frustrated. "It's not like burgers just vanish into thin air."

Mom nodded thoughtfully. "And you're absolutely sure you put it in the fridge?"

"Of course I did!" I snapped, my patience wearing thin. Back in my room, I continued my investigation, this time observing people's reactions. Every time someone mentioned the word *burger*, I studied their faces. Did they look guilty? Surprised? Nervous? I was playing psychological chess, trying to uncover the truth one expression at a time.

Just then, my phone buzzed. It was Billy.

I picked up.

"Hey, Billy."

All I could hear was laughing on the other end. Then his voice came through, thick with sarcasm.

"Detective Tommy! Any luck on your *missing burger (with the bun)*?"

I sighed. "Very funny."

"I think I know what happened to it," he said with mock seriousness. "The lads and I have it. We're saving it for lunch after our game. Or maybe we'll send it back to you, in an Uber!"

I could hear them all cracking up in the background.

I rolled my eyes. "Look, Billy, I'm hanging up."

"Alright, alright, chill. We're just messing around," he said, still chuckling. "But it *is* kind of weird, right? A whole burger just vanishes like that?"

"I KNOW!" I said, exasperated.

"That's what I've been saying!"

As I ended the call, I couldn't help but wonder,

Was Billy joking?

Or did he know something?

I just shrug it off.

The mystery deepens.

A NEW CLUE EMERGES.

I headed downstairs again, not expecting anything new, but my instincts told me to take one more look. I opened the fridge slowly, methodically. This time, with sharp detective eyes sharpened by two days of intense observation, something caught my attention.

There was a **pot**. A medium-sized silver pot, sitting exactly where I had placed my missing burger (with the bun) two days ago.

How had I missed it before?

With all the fuss, the theories, the blame-shifting, the teasing, I had completely overlooked it. The excitement around the case had clearly clouded my usually sharp observation skills. The pot was there, silently suspicious. How long has that been there? *Why didn't anyone mention it, not Mom, not Dad, not even Mylo sniffing around?*

I felt a strange chill down my spine. This was no longer just about a missing burger. This was a *cover-up*.

I raced back upstairs and flopped into my chair, my mind spinning with questions. The case had officially taken a turn. My prime suspect had been Johnny, the midnight fridge raider, but now? I wasn't so sure.

What if it wasn't Johnny?

What if it were *one of my parents?*

I rubbed my temples. "Come on, Tommy, think," I whispered to myself. "You're better than this. You've watched enough detective shows to know that nothing is ever what it seems."

Back in the kitchen, I returned to the scene of the clue. I opened the fridge again, this time with a purpose. I carefully pulled out the mystery pot and placed it on the counter. The pot was cold and slightly damp on the outside. It had clearly been in there for a while.

And then, I saw it: a small, white label stuck neatly to the lid.

"Vegetables: Mon 3:15 PM"

That's Dad's handwriting. No question about it. Dad is known in the family for being obsessively organised with leftovers. Labelled. Dated. Filed in neat rows in the fridge like edible library books.

I lifted the lid slowly.

Steamed vegetables. Broccoli. Carrots. Cauliflower. Green beans. Definitely Dad's style, Mom would've added butter and seasoning. This was pure health food.

I raised an eyebrow and let out a half-chuckle, half-sigh.

So Dad put the pot in the fridge, but did he also move my burger to make room?

And *where* did the burger go?

And *why* didn't he say anything about it?

For two days, we've all been searching, speculating, and accusing, and nobody thought to say, "Hey, who moved the burger so we could fit in this random pot of vegetables?"

It didn't add up.

I stood there, staring into the fridge, piecing it together like a jigsaw puzzle with missing edges. Maybe Mom cooked the veggies and left the pot on the stove, as she often did. Then, as usual, Dad, tidy, practical, methodical Dad, had packed them away. But that still didn't explain what happened to *my burger (with the bun).* Did Dad see it and move it? Did he throw it away, thinking it was old? Or, was he covering for someone else? Suddenly, the case wasn't just about a burger anymore.

It was about *secrecy.*

It was about *betrayal.*

It was about *cold vegetables and unanswered questions.*

Back to square one. The burger was still missing. The pot was just a distraction, or maybe the key clue. I wasn't sure yet.

All I knew was that someone in this house was hiding something.

And I was going to find out who.

WHERE IS THE MISSING BURGER?
(with the bun)

I had to be practical about my investigation. It was time to go old school, interviews. One suspect at a time. And yes, I could confidently rule out Mylo the cat. Though he has the stealth of a ninja and the appetite of a teenage boy, I've observed him closely. He's more interested in warm laps and napping in laundry baskets than in criminal activity, most of the time.

Still, Mylo might prove useful. He's always shadowing me like a furry detective sidekick, and I suspect he's just as invested in solving this case as I am. Maybe it's guilt. I haven't exactly been warm towards him since the Great Burger Incident. Our relationship has been frosty ever since I discovered the empty plate and the single breadcrumb left as a taunt.

Let me be clear: *everyone* is a suspect. During this investigation, I have no friends. No allies. No family. Only the truth. And someone, friend or foe, is going to pay for the disappearance of my burger. Not just any burger, either. The burger. Perfectly seasoned, nestled in its toasted bun, waiting for me in the fridge… and now gone.

As intriguing as the case has become, some obstacles are just too large, like dusting for fingerprints. Our kitchen sees more traffic than a city bus stop. Everyone's fingerprints are everywhere. It wouldn't prove a thing. And anyway, the pot in the fridge, the one I now noticed had mysteriously appeared, may have nothing to do with the theft at all. But still, I can't shake the feeling that I'm missing something. Something small, but important.

Originally, I had my brother Johnny pegged as the prime suspect. But after further thought and observation, I had to let him off the hook. That leaves Onetta. My sister. Clever. Calculating. Occasionally kind. But above all else, unpredictable. If I want this case cracked wide open, I'm going to need her help. The problem? Onetta doesn't come cheap. She's hard to bribe, even harder to impress, and she remembers *everything*. If I ask for her help, I'll owe her. For a very, very long time.

Still, desperate times call for desperate alliances.

I made my way to her room and knocked, heart pounding with cautious optimism.

No answer.

Then, from behind the door, came a sudden shout:

"WHAT do you want!?"

I flinched. "Hi, Onetta… can I talk to you for a minute? Please, sis?"

"I'm playing my game. You'll have to wait 'til I'm done. DO NOT disturb me again. I'll text you."

"Okay, sis," I replied solemnly.

Her voice came back, laced with amusement. "Tommy, drop the 'sis' act. You need something. Be practical."

I could hear the grin in her voice. Great. She already knew I was in trouble. Asking her was either the best idea I ever had, or the worst mistake of my short sleuthing career.

I decided I needed some air. The walls of our house felt like they were closing in on me. I grabbed my notebook and whistled for Mylo.

"I'm going for a walk," I said as I passed her door.

"Take your time," she replied sweetly. "This game's going to take at least an hour."

Was she punishing me on purpose? I stormed outside, frustration bubbling beneath the surface. Why couldn't she just be a helpful big sister for once? But no, this was Onetta. She wasn't going to lift a finger until it benefited her.

I headed toward the park, Mylo trotting beside me like a small, silent bodyguard. We found a quiet bench far from the noise of screaming kids and barking dogs. Mylo doesn't like crowds. Honestly, neither do I right now.

I flipped open my notebook and tried to reset my brain. Starting from scratch. Back to the scene of the crime, mentally, at least.

Then it hit me.

The pot of vegetables. The one I didn't see earlier. Mom made those vegetables on the same day she cooked the burgers. Coincidence? Unlikely. I hate vegetables. But Johnny and Onetta? They love them. So, if one of them wanted some, they'd have to take the pot out of the fridge, right? And to make space, maybe they took out my burger and forgot to put it back in.

And what happens to a forgotten burger left out on the counter? I glanced at Mylo, who stared back at me with his usual blank expression. Innocent, or pretending?

Was he the opportunist who snatched it?

Or was this a two-person job, an accidental accomplice situation?

Alternatively, maybe someone moved the pot, took out the burger to rearrange the fridge, and just never noticed where it landed. But I could rule out Mom. If she'd seen it, she would never have tossed it or fed it to Mylo without asking. She respects food, especially burgers. Sighing, I leaned back on the bench, defeated. I needed help. Real help. I'd have to wait for Onetta to finish her game, even if it meant paying the price later. I let myself enjoy the breeze, just for a moment, and tossed a ball for Mylo.

Some younger kids tried to join in, chasing Mylo around. He hated it, darting behind my legs and giving me a look like, *why do you bring me to places with people?* I gently explained to the kids that he wasn't much of a people-cat, and they moved on.

I checked my phone.

Time had flown.

"Come on, Mylo," I said, rising from the bench and stretching my legs. "It's time. Operation Onetta is a go. We're going to solve this mystery, with or without a bribe."

Mylo didn't look convinced.

But I was ready.

The sleuthing would continue. The case of the missing burger wasn't cold yet.

Arriving back home, I headed straight for the kitchen and grabbed a cold bottle of water from the fridge. The familiar sound of the cap clicking open gave me a small sense of control, one of the few things I had left.

Mom was at the sink, drying some dishes. She glanced over her shoulder and smiled.

"How was your walk, Tommy?"

"It was good," I replied, taking a long drink. "Mylo enjoyed it, too, well, mostly. A bunch of kids tried to play with him, but he wasn't having any of it. You know how he is."

She chuckled softly. "Typical Mylo."

Then, as if she'd been waiting for the right moment, she asked, "Any breakthroughs in the case of your missing burger, with the bun?"

"Not yet," I said, wiping my mouth with the back of my hand. "But I've brought in backup. Onetta's going to help me crack the case."

Mom raised an eyebrow, clearly impressed. "Well, my word. You're really taking this seriously, huh?"

"Of course I am," I said, tightening my grip on the water bottle. "A burger doesn't just vanish into thin air, not *my* burger. It's been two whole days, and there's still no sign of it. No crumbs, no grease marks, no wrappers, *nothing*. And I'm supposed to just forget about it?" I shook my head. "No way. I *need* to find out what happened."

She gave a light shrug, as if it wasn't a big deal. But that shrug, it bugged me.

Why was she so calm about this?

Too calm. Something flickered in her eyes just before she turned back to the sink. Was it amusement? Or, was it guilt? Could she know something? Was she hiding something from me?

I narrowed my eyes slightly. The plot was thickening like old gravy.

Without another word, I bolted upstairs. I needed to prepare myself, mentally and strategically. Onetta was almost done with her game, and if I wanted her on my team, I had to be ready. Interrogations, theories, timelines, I'd need it all. This case was far from over. And somewhere in this house, the truth was waiting.

CHIEF INSPECTOR ONETTA

I stood outside her door, folder in hand, notepad tucked under my arm, heart pounding like I was about to face a courtroom judge.

"Onetta?" I knocked gently, trying not to sound desperate.

"Come in, Tommy. Sit down." Her voice was calm, professional, too professional.

As I stepped into her room, she was already swivelling in her chair, giving me her full attention like an officer ready to interrogate a suspect.

"What do you need my help with?" she asked, folding her arms. I cleared my throat. "Well, my burger, you know, the one that's been missing from the fridge for the past two days? No one's admitted to seeing it. I've searched our fridge and even peeked inside Johnny's mini fridge, but nothing." My voice dropped. "It's like it vanished into thin air."

"Is this the same burger you asked me about yesterday?"

"Yes," I said quietly, the disappointment still raw.

She nodded slowly, then leaned back in her chair. "Alright. So what exactly do you want me to do?"

"I need your help to solve the case. I've already questioned everyone in this house. They all say they don't know anything about the missing burger, with the bun. No confessions. No clues. Just silence."

Onetta paused for a moment, then leaned forward.

"Okay, Tommy. If I'm going to help, I'm going to do this properly. I want full control. From this point on, I am Chief Inspector Onetta. That means you hand over all evidence, all notes, your suspect list, *everything*. Tell me everything you've done so far, and I'll take it from here."

I frowned. "Wait, hold on. I asked for your *help*, not for you to take over completely. I've been on this case for two whole days. I just need a second opinion, a fresh pair of eyes, not a hostile takeover!"

She raised an eyebrow. "Tommy. You've been investigating for *two days* and still don't have a solid lead. You're spinning your wheels. So it's either I take charge, or you continue wasting time. Your choice."

I stared at her, regret starting to creep in. I knew it was a mistake to ask her.

"Give me a few minutes to think," I mumbled, backing out of her room.

"Five minutes," she called after me. "My time is valuable. I'm a very busy person."

I stormed into my room, fuming. She was trying to take over *my* case, my investigation, my mission for justice.

"What should I do, Mylo?" I asked.

Mylo blinked at me from the edge of my bed and let out a soft, "Meow. Meow."

Was that an agreement? Hunger? Indifference? With Mylo, it was impossible to tell.

"You're right," I sighed. "You're my assistant, but we need backup. I'll let her take the lead, for now. She can have the title of Chief Inspector. I still think 'Detective Tommy' sounds cooler anyway."

I took a deep breath, grabbed my evidence folder, notes, sketches, and everything I had gathered so far. This was it.

Returning to Onetta's room, I knocked again.

"Come in, Tommy. Have you made up your mind?"

I entered, reluctantly. "Okay," I said. "You can be the Chief Inspector. But I want updates, every step, every clue, every theory. I still care about this case."

She gave me a sly smile. "Tommy, *I'm* in charge now. You don't give me conditions. You work *for* me. Step back and watch how a professional solves a mystery."

Without another word, she grabbed her laptop, a stack of books, and all the evidence I'd spent two days collecting. She walked out briskly toward the living room.

"I'm setting up my office," she called back. "I'll let you know when I need you."

I watched her go, my arms dangling uselessly by my sides. She was good. I had to admit it. She moved like someone with a plan, with purpose, something I wish I'd thought of. I hadn't even considered setting up an investigation headquarters. I'd just been chasing crumbs, literally and metaphorically.

I felt a little crushed. A little annoyed. But mostly, I just really wanted to know what happened to my burger.

If she could solve the case, then she could keep her fancy title. Because justice mattered more than pride.

And I had a feeling that, with Chief Inspector Onetta on the case, the truth wouldn't stay hidden for long.

About an hour later, I heard my name echo through the house.

"Tommy!"

I jumped up and bolted down the stairs so fast I nearly tripped over Mylo, who hissed and darted out of my path. I was out of breath by the time I reached the living room.

"Did you solve it already?" I asked, panting.

"Please tell me you found the culprit!"

Onetta rolled her eyes. "Don't be silly, Tommy. This isn't a cartoon. I'm conducting the first official interview." She had completely transformed the front room into her makeshift office. She was seated behind Dad's computer desk, which she had tidied up and repositioned to face the rest of the room like some kind of courtroom bench. A single chair sat opposite her, an interrogation seat.

"**S**it down," she said, motioning to the chair in front of her with all the authority of a real chief inspector.
I hesitated. "What is this about?"

"You," she said simply. "You're the first person I'm interviewing."

"Me?!" I almost shouted. "But it's *my* burger that's missing! Why should *I* be interviewed?"
Onetta didn't even flinch. "Enough with the shouting, Tommy. Calm down. This is a proper investigation, and every investigator worth their salt knows you always start close to the case. You're the one who reported it. That makes you the first person to rule out or rule in. It's standard procedure."

"But I'm the victim!" I protested. "That burger, with the bun, meant a lot to me! You can't honestly think *I* took it."

"I don't think anything yet," she said coolly. "That's why I'm interviewing everyone. If you still want my help solving this case, then you need to follow the rules. No exceptions."
I crossed my arms and glared at her. I couldn't believe this. She was turning this into some kind of TV detective drama.

"Chief Inspector Onetta," I said sarcastically, "you've got a lot of nerve interviewing *me*, after *I* brought this case to you!"

She leaned forward, hands clasped like a real interrogator. "If you're going to start questioning my methods, maybe you'd prefer to take the case back and solve it yourself?"

I groaned, knowing she had me. "Fine," I said, voice low and gravelly. "Sorry, Chief Inspector."

She gave a satisfied nod. "Good. Now that we're done with the dramatics, let's begin. Time is ticking, and the truth won't wait."

I reluctantly sank into the interrogation chair, folding my arms and slouching a little. This wasn't how I had pictured things going when I asked for her help. I thought she'd look at the clues, maybe point out something I'd missed, not accuse *me*.

Still, if this was what it took to find out what happened to my beloved, perfectly crafted burger (with the bun), I was willing to do it.

Even if it meant being treated like a suspect.

She opened her notebook and clicked her pen. "State your full name, please."

I sighed. "You already know my name."

"*State it,*" she repeated firmly, hiding a smirk.

"Tommy. Just Tommy."

"Date and time of the last known sighting of the burger?"

I stared at her. "You're really doing this, huh?"

"Answer the question."

"Two days ago. Around 3 p.m. I put the burger in the fridge after lunch. I was saving it for dinner."

"Did anyone see you put it there?"

"No, I don't think so. But Mylo was in the kitchen. He saw everything."

She scribbled something in her notebook. "Noted. And did you check on it later that day?"

"I didn't need to. I *knew* it was there. It was in a clear container, on the top shelf. I even wrote my name on the lid with a permanent marker!"

"Hmm. Anything else you remember? Any smells? Sounds? Suspicious fridge movements?"

I blinked at her. "Suspicious, fridge movements?"

She grinned. "Just checking."

Despite myself, I smiled a little. She might be bossy, but she was thorough.

"Alright, Tommy," she said, closing her notebook with a snap. "You're officially ruled out, for now."

"For *now*?" I asked.

"Hey, a good inspector never assumes anything until all the evidence is in. You may be innocent, or you may be clever."

I stood up, rolling my eyes. "I should've never given you that title."

She leaned back in Dad's creaky desk chair. "And yet, you did. Now, send Johnny in. It's time for the next suspect."

As I walked out, I couldn't help but feel both annoyed *and* impressed. She was taking this more seriously than I ever expected.

And maybe, just maybe, that meant we were finally getting closer to the truth.

THE INTERVIEWS

It all began with a missing burger. Not just any burger, *my* burger. The one I'd carefully saved, wrapped in a paper plate, sealed in a clear plastic bag, and placed on the third shelf of the fridge, right-hand side. The one with the perfect bun. It was gone.

That's when my sister transformed into Chief Inspector Onetta.

She sat at the kitchen table, her phone propped up like an official recording device, her glasses perched low on her nose for dramatic effect.

"Tell me, Tommy," she began in her best detective voice, "when was the last time you saw the burger, with the bun?"

I rolled my eyes but played along, for now. "Let me think... I had the burgers on Monday evening, when Mom"..

"Stop right there!" she snapped, holding up her hand. "Just the facts. Not who cooked them. This is not a cooking show."

"Onetta," I sighed, "you're taking this way out of context. What facts do you want? I'm giving you the whole picture, how it started"

"I *said* facts, not commentary," she cut in, pressing the record button. "Now, again from the top."
She tapped her phone. "Interview commencing. Timer set. Recorder rolling."
I took a deep breath. "Fine. The last time I saw my burger, *with the bun*, was Monday evening."

"Good," she nodded. "And what time exactly?"

"Around 19:00 hours," I said, trying not to laugh at her seriousness.

"Proceed. What did you do with the burger?"
I clenched my jaw. Why had I ever asked her for help? I should've known she'd turn this into a full-blown interrogation. Still, I kept my cool or at least pretended to.

"I placed the burger in the fridge. Right-hand side, third shelf from the top. It was on a white paper plate, wrapped in a clear plastic bag. That was the last time I saw the poor, unfortunate thing."
I gave her a mock bow. "Anything else, *Madam Chief Inspector*?"
I turned to leave, but her voice stopped me mid-step.

"Tommy! I didn't dismiss you. Come back. The interview is not complete."

"I'm thirsty," I said with a fake yawn. "Interrogations are hard work."

"Fine," she said, unimpressed. "Bring me a glass of water while you're at it."

"Please", I said.

"Okay, please, hurry up now, Tommy!".

I fetched her the glass and handed it over with exaggerated courtesy. "Anything else, Madam?" I asked, drenched in sarcasm.

She narrowed her eyes. "Sarcasm is beyond you, Tommy. Don't try it. You are dismissed, *for now*. But don't go too far. I may need to bring you back in."

"Oh, my word," I muttered under my breath. "What have I done? I've created a monster."

Fuming, I stomped upstairs to my room. Of *course,* she had taken over the entire investigation. I was supposed to be running this! Instead, I'd become suspect number one in my own case. Ridiculous. Who hides a burger, then eats it, then files a missing food report on themselves? Not me.

But apparently, that was Onetta's theory.

She even had the nerve to say, "I have to rule you out as a suspect." Me. A suspect. In my own missing burger case.

I tossed myself onto my bed and tried to distract my mind with games on my phone. It didn't help much. Now and then, I could hear her voice downstairs, interviewing the others. Mom. Dad. Even Auntie Paulette, who wasn't even home Monday night.

It felt like hours before she finally called me again.

"Tommy!"

No way I was giving her the satisfaction of rushing down like her personal assistant. Instead, I called her.

"I'm on my way," I said coolly, stalling another minute just to make her wait.

When I finally arrived, she was fuming.

"Sorry, I was busy," I said.

"Busy? Doing what, Tommy?" she barked. "Playing games on your phone? You *asked* me to assist you. I took time out of *my* busy schedule to help, and this is how you treat me?"

"Okay, okay, calm down," I muttered, avoiding her glare.

"Here's the update," she said, regaining her composure and flipping through her notes. "I've interviewed three suspects. I may need to re-interview one or two. Only Johnny remains. He's due home late tonight. I'll catch him first thing in the morning."

She leaned back, smugly satisfied. "We're making progress. By tomorrow, I'll wrap this case. You'll know *exactly* who took your precious burger, with the bun."

"Can't wait," I mumbled, then turned to head back upstairs. Still annoyed. Still burger-less.

This wasn't over.

INTERROGATION ESCALATE

The next morning, I slept in, more like sulked in. By the time I finally dragged myself out of bed, it was early afternoon. But I wasn't excited to face the day. Not because I was lazy, but because the case I had started, *my* case, had been hijacked by none other than Chief Inspector Onetta.

We were supposed to be partners.

I shuffled down the hallway and immediately heard voices coming from the front room. Loud voices. Especially Johnny's.

"Why are you asking me questions about this stupid burger?" he barked. "I already told Mom and Dad, I didn't take it!"

"You're making a big deal out of nothing. Who even cares about Tommy's burger? He probably ate it himself and now wants Mom to feel sorry for him so she'll cook him more!"

I peeked around the corner but stayed out of sight.

"Look, Johnny," Onetta said calmly, "someone took the missing burger, with the bun. Everyone I've interviewed so far has denied taking it. So, unless the burger grew legs and walked out of the fridge, or Mylo the cat has developed a taste for seasoned beef, *someone is lying.*"

"I don't have time for this nonsense!" Johnny shouted. "I've got things to do before I leave for work. I'm not standing here listening to this. I already told you, I didn't take it!"

Then he turned on her.

"What about you, sis?" he snapped. "Did you take it? Who's going to interview *you*? Or does Chief Inspector Onetta think she's above the law?"

Now *that* got my attention.

I stepped into the room. "Afternoon," I said casually.

Johnny was storming out, eyes blazing. "Was this your idea?" he asked, jabbing a finger at me.

"Nope. All Onetta," I said with a shrug.

"Count me out," he muttered. "I've got better things to do."

I turned to Onetta, suppressing a grin. "Chief Inspector," I said, "may I have a word with you?"

She raised an eyebrow, suspicious.

"What is it, Tommy?"

I sat down across from her, folding my arms. "I've decided, it's *your* turn. I'm going to interview you now. After all, I'm still part of this investigation. And as your fellow detective, I have every right to question *you*."

She scoffed. "There's no need for that. You know I don't eat burgers."

"That's not the point. Everyone's a suspect. Even Chief Inspectors."

She leaned back in her chair and crossed her arms. "Fine. Let's get it over with."

"Gladly," I said, slipping into full detective mode.

I reached into my pocket and pulled out an old pair of reading glasses I found in Mom's room. I perched them on my nose and adjusted them dramatically.

"What are you wearing?" Onetta asked, chuckling.

"Please address me properly," I said. "Detective Tommy, if you don't mind. And no more interruptions, I ask the questions here."

She rolled her eyes but nodded. "Fine. Detective Tommy. Proceed."

I flipped open a small notebook and began scribbling nonsense symbols just to look important. I cleared my throat.

"Where were you at approximately 19:00 hours on Monday evening?"

"In the kitchen. Helping Mom clean up," she said, unamused.

"Interesting," I said, jotting that down. "And were you alone?"

"No. Mom was there. And Dad came in later."

"Hmm," I said, squinting dramatically at my notebook. "And what's your relationship with burgers?"

"I *don't* eat them, Tommy. I'm more of a chicken-nugget person."

"Yet you live in a house full of burger lovers."

"That's not a crime," she snapped.

"Not yet," I said, tapping my pen thoughtfully.

She laughed. "You're ridiculous."

I held up my hand. "Interview's not over, Chief. Just one more question: Have you, at any point, opened the fridge and noticed the burger was missing?"

"Yes. But I figured someone ate it."

"Interesting. Thank you for your cooperation."

Just as I closed my notebook, Onetta sat forward. "Detective Tommy," she said mockingly, "let's meet again in about two hours. I'll update you on my progress, and you can share your *findings.*"

"Copy that, Chief," I said, standing tall. But just as I reached the door, I heard her call Johnny's name again.

"Johnny," she said from the living room, "please step into the interview room. And close the door."

I paused and backtracked, slowly, stealthily, then pressed my ear against the door.

From what I could make out, Johnny was not in the mood.

"I already told you I didn't take the stupid burger!" he barked. "I told Mom, I told Dad, now I've told you. That's enough!"

"Johnny," Onetta said coolly, "just answer the questions."

"I don't *have* time for this! I'm going to be late for the gym!"

Things were heating up. Johnny sounded furious. Onetta, of course, remained calm, which only made him angrier. The house felt like a crime show now, with interviews, suspects, and rising tension.

But one thing was clear:

The truth was still hiding somewhere, and the burger thief was getting nervous.

SUSPICIONS AND SOLITUDE

"No one is above suspicion," said Inspector Onetta firmly. "You claim you didn't take the burger, with the bun, so why are you so angry?" She paused. "Just answer the questions, and then you're free to go."

From where I was eavesdropping near the front room door, I heard Johnny's voice rising again, louder, and this time slower, as if he was trying to control his temper, but failing miserably.

"I… *PAUSED*… did not… *PAUSED*… take… *PAUSED*… his stupid burger, with the bun!" he exploded.

He was fuming. I couldn't hear every word, but I caught the tone, pure rage. Onetta asked him a few more questions after that, but their voices had dipped too low for me to catch the details. Then I heard her voice again, this time clear and clipped: "This interview is now terminated. Time: 14:00 hours. You are free to go.

"Footsteps approached.

Panicked, I darted away from the door and bolted into the kitchen, nearly tripping over Mylo in the process.

That was too close. It wasn't Johnny coming out; it was our parents heading downstairs. The last thing I needed was to get caught spying on Onetta's makeshift crime lab. A loud slam echoed through the house. The front door. Johnny had stormed out, muttering something under his breath that I couldn't make out. But based on his body language and attitude, he was not happy. I scribbled a mental note: *Possible suspect, highly defensive, quick to anger. Will report to the Chief Inspector.*

As for the next interviews, it was time for Mom and Dad to be questioned again. Onetta had mentioned earlier that she might recall one or two suspects for further clarification. I tried to linger close enough to listen, but Mylo was now demanding my attention, circling my legs and meowing loudly.

"Alright, alright," I said, scooping him up. "Let's go for a walk, Agent Mylo."

I headed upstairs, grabbed a cardigan, just in case, along with my phone and headphones. Even though it was summer, the wind had picked up and made the afternoon feel cooler. Still, a walk would help me clear my mind. Sometimes, fresh air and movement help connect the dots in a mystery. Mylo trotted beside me as we made our way down the street toward the park. It was lively as usual. Families were out enjoying the sunshine, some packing up to leave as the sun dipped lower in the sky. A couple of kids ran over to pet Mylo, but, in typical Mylo fashion, he swerved dramatically out of reach like a seasoned escape artist. He's not a fan of strangers. Or children. Or really, anyone other than me and Mom.

As we wandered further into the park, I found a quiet bench tucked under a tree and sat down, away from the noisy laughter and screaming toddlers. Mylo hopped up beside me and curled into a loaf shape, purring softly.

"You know, Mylo," I said, rubbing his head, "it's kind of ironic. One minute the burger's there, safe and sound in the fridge, next minute, poof! Gone without a trace."

He blinked up at me but said nothing. Not even a polite *meow*.

"It's weird, right?" I continued. "A whole burger. *With the bun*. Wrapped. Bagged. On the third shelf. And no one knows anything?"

I shook my head, watching the wind rustle the trees.

"This is a strange phenomenon, Mylo. Burgers don't just vanish into thin air. It's like we're living in some weird food-based episode of *Sherlock Holmes*."

Mylo blinked again and turned his head away to stare at a passing squirrel. Typical. I leaned back and exhaled. "I just hope Onetta figures this out. I really do. She's acting all professional and in control, but what if she's too professional? What if she's *pretending* not to care about burgers just to throw us off?"

I looked down at Mylo. "You think she could be hiding her guilt?"

He didn't respond, clearly more interested in grooming his paw than cracking the case.

I let the thought sit in the breeze. Could Onetta be that clever? That manipulative? Or was she truly innocent, just a sister with a badge and a superiority complex?

Either way, this mystery wasn't over.

And I was going to see it through, even if I had to interrogate every member of the family again, including the cat.

THE INVESTIGATION DEEPENS

Looking down at my phone, I suddenly realised the time.

"Come on, Mylo!" I said, leaping up from the park bench. He blinked lazily at me but followed, tail swishing in protest as we hurried back home.

Once inside, I made a quick detour to the bathroom, nature calls, even for detectives, and then headed straight to my room to drop off my things. A few minutes later, I walked down the hallway and knocked lightly on Onetta's door. No response.

I knocked again, louder this time. Still nothing.

I hesitated, then slowly pushed the door open and peeked in. The room was empty. No Onetta. Just her neatly made bed and a slightly ominous bulletin board with strings and photos she must've pinned up for "evidence." Classic Onetta.

I spun around and jogged downstairs. Sure enough, there she was, sitting stiffly at the desk in the front room, notebook in hand, eyes glued to her phone like she was monitoring a live security feed.

"You're fifteen minutes late, Tommy," she said without even looking up. "I don't tolerate tardiness."

I rolled my eyes but offered a half-hearted smile. "Apologies, Chief. The walk took longer than I planned, and Mylo insisted on sniffing every leaf along the way."

Onetta finally looked up, her eyes narrowed like a hawk circling its prey. "Let's get started," she said, her voice crisp. "From my findings so far, here's what we know."

She flipped open her notebook like it held the secrets of the universe.

"You placed your burger, with the bun, on the third shelf, right side of the fridge, wrapped on a white paper plate, inside a clear plastic bag. At that time, there was *no* pot of vegetables in the fridge."

She paused dramatically.

"So, who put the pot of vegetables in there?"

"Mom did," I replied, trying to sound confident but sensing a trap.

"Correct," said Chief Inspector Onetta, tapping her pen on the notebook. According to Mom's statement, she added the pot of vegetables *after* you placed the burger. She also said she had to move things around to make space, but she doesn't recall seeing the burger."

She leaned back slightly, a sly smile tugging at the corner of her mouth. "So, the timeline narrows. The burger went missing either *before* the pot was added, or *after*, when she was rearranging things."

She folded her arms and stared at me.

"What's your theory, Inspector Tommy?" she asked, her tone half-serious, half-mocking.

I ignored her smug grin. "Well," I said, tapping my chin thoughtfully, "if Mom had to shift things around, that means she interacted with the shelf. She should have seen the burger, but she didn't. That could mean one of two things: the burger was already gone, or something distracted her from noticing it."

"Distraction?" she said, raising an eyebrow.

"Maybe Mylo jumped on the counter, or the phone rang, or she was just in a rush. It happens. But it doesn't rule her out as a suspect," I added, half-joking.

She scoffed. "Tommy, our mother is not a criminal."

"She's also a fantastic cook. Maybe she took pity on Dad and gave *him* the burger," I offered with a grin.

Onetta shook her head but was clearly enjoying the debate. "Don't jump to conclusions. Let's stay with the facts. Whoever took the burger knew exactly where it was and wanted it enough to take it without asking."

"Which brings us back to Johnny," I muttered. "He had motive, opportunity, and attitude."

"True," she agreed. "But I'm not crossing anyone off the list just yet. Even *you* aren't fully in the clear."

"**Me**?" I gasped. "This is *my* burger we're talking about!"

"And I wouldn't put it past you to eat it, forget about it, and create this entire dramatic investigation for sympathy," she said matter-of-factly.

I stared at her, offended. "That's actually possible," I admitted reluctantly. "But highly unlikely."

She smirked. "Well, I've got one more suspect to cross-examine before I close this case."

My heart skipped. "Who?"

She didn't answer. Instead, she picked up her phone, pressed play, and a familiar voice crackled through the speaker, Dad's.

"Wait, you *recorded* the interviews?" I asked.

Onetta looked up. "Of course. Proper case documentation."

I folded my arms. "This is becoming a full-blown trial, isn't it?"

"**O**nly if we find out someone perjured themselves over a burger," she said calmly, and turned her attention back to the recording.

She could've taken it out and forgotten to put it back, or maybe she just placed it on a different shelf," I suggested, half-thinking aloud.

"Possibly," said Onetta, tapping her pen against her notebook. "She did mention rotating some items in the fridge to make room for the pot of vegetables."

She flipped a page. "But here's what's odd: Dad also said *he* moved things around in the fridge later that same day. My question is, why? Why did he need to rearrange stuff again if Mom already made space?"

I frowned. "That *is* strange. Sounds like we've got overlapping fridge activity."

"I think," Onetta said, leaning forward with a glint of certainty in her eyes, "this case is down to Mom or Dad."

"Not Mom," I said quickly, shaking my head. "She's not a burger person, and she *knows* that burger was mine. If she saw it, she would've wrapped it better, maybe even labelled it with my name. That's just how she is. So my bet? Dad."

Onetta smirked. "I think we're finally on the same page."

"I mean, think about it," I said, warming up to the theory. "Dad always packs a mountain of food for work, fruits, snacks, a random boiled egg here and there, and half the time he brings it all back untouched. It's entirely possible he scooped the burger up by mistake and forgot about it."

"Let's face facts," Onetta added, checking her notes. "We've been searching for two days straight. We've turned the fridge inside out, conducted multiple interviews, and still no one's admitted to seeing or eating the burger, with the bun. Everyone claims innocence. Even *you*," she said, narrowing her eyes at Mylo, who blinked back at her without a shred of guilt.

"What about Johnny?" I asked. "He was pretty hostile during your interview. And Mom said he didn't take it, but let's be real, Johnny wouldn't bother with the bun. He's all about protein."

"Exactly," Onetta nodded. "One burger isn't enough for Johnny, and he avoids carbs like the plague. But still, he *could* have taken the patty and chucked the bun in the bin."

I raised an eyebrow. "Is that what your detective instinct tells you?"

She shrugged. "Maybe. But I've ruled him out based on attitude and alibi. He didn't even go near the kitchen that morning, according to Dad."

"And Mom only ever makes burgers for Johnny and me," I said. "If she *had* seen the burger, she would've saved it for me, maybe put it on the top shelf or something. Which leaves us with one suspect",

"Dad," we both said at the same time.

Just then, a familiar voice boomed from the kitchen.

"Tommy! Onetta! Come here quick!"

It was Dad.

We jumped up and rushed toward the kitchen, Mylo padding behind us curiously. Dad was standing by the fridge, the door wide open.

"Look here," he said, pointing toward the bottom left shelf. "Here's your missing burger, with the bun."

Mom came in behind us, looking shocked. "Where did you find it, James?"

"It was wedged under the back of the shelf," Dad replied, frowning. "Tucked behind the yoghurt containers. It must've been pushed all the way to the back."

Mom shook her head. "That's odd. I've checked that fridge three times. I even moved things around to make room for the pot and still didn't see any sign of it."

"Same," I said, peering inside. "It's like it just... reappeared."

Onetta stepped forward with her classic investigative face. "Let me see the missing burger," she said.

Dad handed it to her.

She inspected it carefully, holding it between two fingers like it were radioactive. The bun was flattened, the lettuce limp, and the patty looked like it had aged ten years in two days.

"It looks, traumatised," I said.

Onetta passed it to me. "As Chief Inspector of this case," she said solemnly, "I can confirm this is the long-lost burger. But let me say this—I don't believe for a second that it just *magically* reappeared. We've searched that fridge multiple times. Thoroughly. In both fridges. There was no sign of this burger."

She looked at all of us. "Which leads me to one of two conclusions: either the burger grew wings, flew away on a brief vacation, and returned home out of guilt, or someone took it out, forgot they took it, and then quietly placed it back when they thought no one would notice."

She turned slowly, eyes narrowing at Dad. "So, Mr James, anything you'd like to confess?"

Dad laughed nervously. "I swear I don't remember touching it. But I *did* clean out my lunch bag this morning and found a bag with something squished at the bottom. I might've thought it was an old sandwich..."

"You *took it to work!*" I exclaimed.

"I didn't eat it!" he protested. "I must've mistaken it for something else, forgot about it, and brought it back by accident."

"Case closed," Onetta declared. "Mystery of the Missing Burger, with the bun, solved."

We all stared at the sad, squashed burger in my hand. Mylo finally gave a loud, unimpressed *meow*, then strutted out of the room like he'd known all along.

THE FINDINGS

"**Mr** James," said Onetta, arms folded, and voice cool with certainty, "I believe you took the burger, with the bun, to work by mistake, then forgot about it. When you got home and heard Tommy asking about his missing burger two days in a row, you quietly found it buried in your lunch bag, panicked, and tried to sneak it back into the fridge, shoving it under the shelf, hoping we'd believe it had been there all along."

She paused, lifting the sad, squashed burger in its clingfilm wrapping. "Just look at this thing. It's flat, sad, and looks like it's been through a war. Mom even said she searched every corner of the fridge and saw nothing."

"I agree with that explanation," I said, nodding firmly. Even Mylo chimed in with a perfectly timed "Meow! Meow!", as if offering his own feline verdict.

Dad frowned, shifting uncomfortably. "Why are you all ganging up on me?" he asked, trying to sound offended, but the guilt was written all over his face.

"That's my final conclusion, Tommy," said Onetta, closing her notebook. "It's the only plausible explanation that fits all the evidence. The missing burger case is officially solved."

She turned to me with a smirk. "Now, what are you going to do with the recovered burger, with the bun?"

I stared down at it, holding it between two fingers like it might bite. "Honestly? This thing isn't even fit for Mylo anymore."

Mylo took one look, blinked slowly, and turned his back to it, curling into a nap without a sound. Case closed.

Dad was still muttering to himself in the corner, clearly disappointed that his "hero moment" had backfired. "I mean, I *found* it, didn't I? That should count for something…"

"To be fair," I said, shrugging, "I did suspect you. You always pack too much for work, and Mom backed that theory. Most of the time, you bring stuff back untouched. You probably just threw the burger in your bag and forgot about it."

Onetta nodded. "Exactly. That explains why no one could find it and why it reappeared like a guilty conscience."

Mom sighed, her hands on her hips.

"Personally, I'm just relieved this whole thing is over. You two have been acting like detectives from a crime show. But honestly, you made a great team. Maybe you should work together more often."

"Thanks, Mom," I said. "But I'm still annoyed I never got to eat that burger."

I held it up one last time. "This belongs in the bin."
Dad leaned over. "Don't be so hasty. We don't know how long it was out of the fridge",

"Exactly," I interrupted.

"That's *why* it's going in the bin."

"Don't worry, sweetheart," Mom said warmly, placing a hand on my shoulder.

"I'll make you fresh ones tonight for dinner. And this time, you can have all four. No sharing required."
I lit up.

"Thanks, Mom. You really are the greatest."
She smiled while Onetta packed up her notes, and Mylo finally stretched and wandered off, now that justice had been served.
Dad gave a sheepish shrug and whispered, "Sorry, kid. I owe you one burger, with a bun."
I laughed. "Make it two."

THE FAMILY POST EXCLUSIVE:

MYSTERY OF THE MISSING BURGER SOLVED:

By Chief Inspector Onetta | Special Contributor
Location: The Kitchen
Date Closed: Friday, 4:00 PM
Case File: #BUEGER-2025

After an exhaustive 72-hour investigation, filled with interviews, suspicion, denial, and one unusually quiet cat, the infamous case of the Missing Burger (with the bun) has finally been solved.

Suspect: Mr James (Dad)
Charges: Accidental food misplacement and fridge tampering
Hero (s): Chief Inspector Onetta and Detective Tommy

Silent Witness: Mylo the cat

SUMMARY OF EVENTS:

- Victim (Tommy) placed the burger (with bun) in the fridge.
- Burger mysteriously vanished.
- Interviews conducted with all household members (and one cat).
- Fridge searched no less than **six times**.
- Suspicions pointed to Dad due to food-hoarding habits and suspicious mumbling.
- Burger rediscovered flattened and lifeless under the fridge shelf.
- Dad claims to have "found" it, but the evidence suggests otherwise.
- Burger deemed inedible and respectfully discarded.
- Mom promises reparations in the form of four freshly made burgers, no sharing required.

Official Statement from Chief Inspector Onetta:

"This case tested our patience, our teamwork, and our ability to sniff out the truth (even when it smelled like old lettuce). I'm proud of our detective unit, especially Mylo, for being present and emotionally indifferent throughout."

Comment from Detective Tommy:

"Justice was served: even if my burger wasn't."
CASE STATUS: CLOSED

NEXT CASE: The Mystery of the Missing Cat?
Suspect: Mylo, the cat, once again?

THE END

www.ingramcontent.com/pod-product-compliance
Lightning Source LLC
Chambersburg PA
CBHW021935170626
46807CB00007B/3122